This book belongs to:

_____

MESSAGE TO PARENTS

This book is perfect for parents and children to read aloud together. First read the story to your child. When you read it again run your finger under each line, stopping at each picture for your child to "read." Help your child to work out the picture. If your child makes a mistake, be encouraging as you say the right word. Point out the written word beneath each picture in the margin on the page. Soon your child will be "reading" aloud with you, and at the same time learning the symbols that stand for words.

Conceived by
Deborah Shine

Design by
Canard Design, Inc.

First published in the United States of America by Checkerboard Press, Inc.
Copyright © 1988 Checkerboard Press, Inc.
All rights reserved.

The Three Bears

A **Let's learn to read** Book

Retold by Cindy West

Illustrated by Jill Dubin

Brown Watson

ENGLAND

three

bear

bear

bear

house

woods

Once upon a time there were

 bears: a big Father , a

middle-sized Mother , and

a little Baby . They all lived

in a in the middle of the .

One morning Father 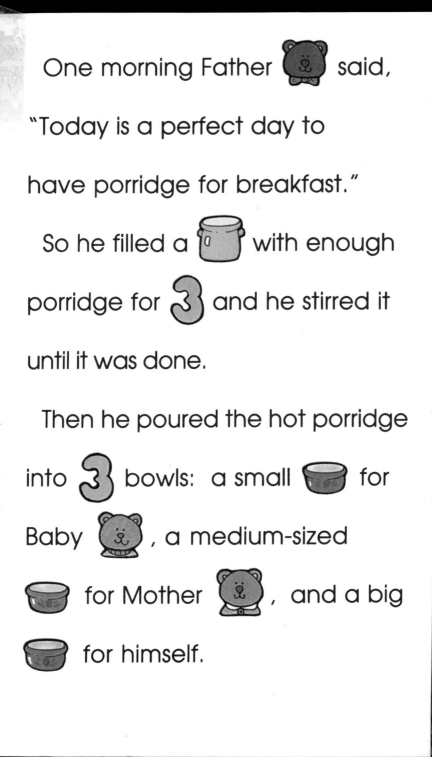 said,

"Today is a perfect day to

have porridge for breakfast."

So he filled a 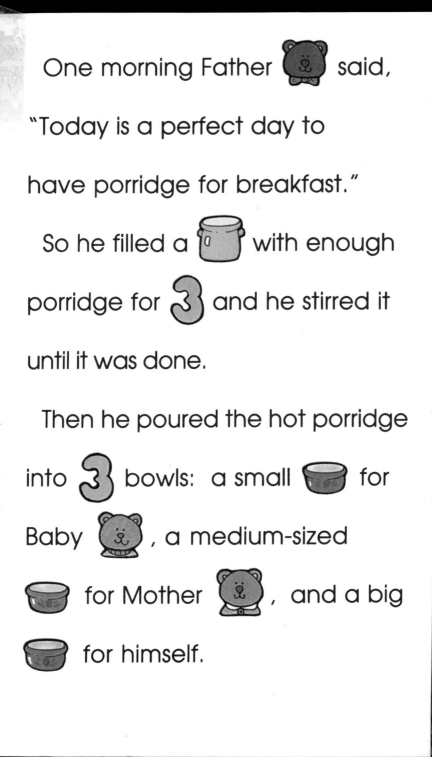 with enough

porridge for 3 and he stirred it

until it was done.

Then he poured the hot porridge

into 3 bowls: a small for

Baby , a medium-sized

 for Mother , and a big

 for himself.

pot

bowl

bear

spoon

bear

woods

Baby picked up his

and took a taste. "This is too hot,"

he complained, and put down

his .

"Our porridge needs time to

cool," said Mother . "Let's

go for a walk in the . When

we get back, our porridge will be

just right."

So they put on their s,

closed the , and went into

the . Just then a little girl

called  walked up to their

. She had been picking

in the , and she felt tired.

coat

door

Goldilocks

house

flowers

Goldilocks

house

When saw the little ,

she thought, "I'm sure these kind

people will let me rest here."

 knocked on the , but

nobody came.

She knocked on the

again, and still nobody came.

door

She opened the  and walked into the . When smelled the porridge, she said, "Hmm, that smells good!"

She picked up a and tasted the porridge in the great big . "Ooh, this is too hot," she said.

spoon

bowl

Goldilocks

bowl

 took a taste from the

middle-sized  . "This is much

too cold," she said with a sigh.

Then she took a taste from the

little  . "Ah! This is just right,"

she said, and she ate it all up!

Then  saw **3** comfortable s. "I'm so tired,"  said, and sat on the great big .

"This  is too high!" she said.

Then she sat down on the middle-sized . "This  is much too low," she said with a sigh.

3
three

chair

Then she sat on the little .

"This is just right!" She smiled. But

 sat down so hard, the

broke into a hundred pieces!

"Ouch!" groaned .

Chair

Goldilocks

Next walked into the bedroom. She saw **3** beds in a row.

slipped off her and lay down on the great big .

"Oh, this is too hard," she said.

three

shoes

bed

bed

Next she lay down on the

middle-sized . "This is much

too soft," she said with a sigh.

Then she lay down on the little

. "This is just right." She

smiled and fell fast asleep.

Just then the  3 bears came home. They were very hungry after their walk. When Father 🐻 picked up his 🥄 he growled, "SOMEONE HAS BEEN EATING MY PORRIDGE!"

three

bear

spoon

bear

spoon

bear

Mother  picked up her  and said, "Someone has been eating my porridge!"

And Baby  whispered, "Someone has been eating my porridge and has eaten it all up!"

Then Father  saw his .

"SOMEONE HAS BEEN SITTING IN

MY !" he growled.

"Someone has been sitting in

my ," said Mother .

"Someone has been sitting in my

 ," squeaked Baby ,

"and it's all broken!"

Then the 3 very unhappy

bears walked upstairs to their

bedroom.

bear

chair

3
three

bed

bear

bear

bear

Goldilocks

three

"SOMEONE HAS BEEN SLEEPING IN MY !" growled Father .

"Someone has been sleeping in my ," said Mother .

"Someone has been sleeping in my ," shouted Baby , "and here she is!"

His angry voice woke  up.

When she saw the bears glaring at her, she jumped out of

, raced down the ,

and out the front  !

And never ever went back

to the 3 bears' again!

stairs

door

house